MW01094509

Tigger the Mouse And The Smithsonians

Nicole Mangum

ISBN: 978-1-960853-34-9

Liberation's Publishing LLC ~ West Point, Mississippi

Let everything that has breathe Praise The Lord
Psalm 150:6

Table of Contents

Jacqueline

Misty, the governess of the house, would turn into mist if she ever knew mice lived in Palouse Manor. A governess is a woman who has been hired to tutor children in their home. Misty prefers that title. She doesn't like the word nanny. It sounds too much like nana, and she isn't even a mother yet. Misty is a great teacher, but she is not fond of farm animals, especially mice. I'm baby Smith, short for Smithsonian. My papa, Papa Smith, was given the name Smithsonian by his great, great papa. Great Papa Smith lived in one of the Smithsonian Institute museums. The Smithsonian Institute is a group  of museums and libraries ran by the United States of America.

We Smiths have lived in Palouse Manor for years now. We were brought here to protect the manor and keep mice away, especially roof rats. We are exceptionally good at our job. We must be, because it gets cold here in Palouse Washington and mice and rodents are always needing shelter in the winter.

Olivia, the only child of the manor, is our favorite human friend. She possesses, or has, an incredibly special gift. She can hear and talk to animals. If she listens that is. I'll tell you about the first time she heard us Smiths later.

We Smithsonians have a covenant, a special promise, never to take the life of any of the mice or rats that find their way into Palouse Manor. We give them notice and time to leave the manor on their own. They can make their homes in the large fields that surround the manor.

Tigger was just a little pup when we first saw him. He was so small, no bigger than a pea. He and his mom, Jacqueline, were the first mice allowed to live in the manor. They were quite the exception.

Jacqueline was different. She had found so much favor with Olivia. She was Olivia's favorite pet next to Smidge the Mangalitsa pig. Jacqueline lived in the manor for a year before Misty found out she was

there. Misty was on a rampage. She set out mouse traps and poisoned pellets. She even went as far as calling the exterminator. We tried desperately to hide Jacqueline from it all. Jacqueline was very distraught. She was so upset on the brink of passing out. She would not have Tigger to leave the manor.

Jacqueline would not take her son with her into the fields. She wouldn't have him living a life fighting off snakes, tomcats, and worst of all barn owls. She had come from such a life. She knew how dangerous it was. She had lost Tigger's dad, Jonathan, to the hard life of living in the fields. This is her story.

It started during the winter moves; the winter moves happen when the weather changes from fall to winter. Most animals move into shelter. Some go into hibernation. Hibernation is when animals seek shelter to sleep through the cold winter months. Some go into shelter underground

or into abandoned buildings. Some go into shelter in the homes of humans.

Tigger's parents, Jacqueline, and Jonathon found shelter in an abandoned barn a few miles away from Palouse Manor. It was on a large farm that hadn't been used for years. The farmhouse was all rickety and falling apart. The barn was the only building worth taking shelter in.

It was early in the year when the barn owl attacked Jonathon. Barn owls' mate around that time and gather food for their mates during courtship. Neither Jonathon nor Jacqueline had noticed their arrival, two barn owls.

Jonathan and Jacqueline had been in the barn for weeks, and it seemed like they would be safe there throughout the winter. They did not have a huge stock of food, so Jonathon would go out every day to search the barn for more.

One day Jonathan noticed a nest in the loft of the barn while searching the barn for food. It looked abandoned, so he didn't feel the need to tell Jacqueline it was there. He stumbled upon a stash of food and was excited. It had been days since his and Jacqueline's last meal. He had no idea, neither did he stop to think that the storage of food belonged to a barn owl. Once he grabbed the piece of dried apple it was too late. He was spotted.

Barn owls were dreadful looking creatures to mice. Their heads bobbled and weaved back and forth looking totally disconnected from their body. Their large dark eyes appear to pierce through you. They're quick! Once they spot you it's over. they hardly ever miss their target, even in total darkness.

Jonathan made a dash for it. He ran because he knew his life depended on it. He skipped the ladder altogether leaping from the loft to the barn floor. He landed with a thud dropping the apple which was too heavy to carry any longer.

Swoosh! He heard the barn owl swoop down after him. His heart seemed to have stopped, then pounded out of his chest. All he could think of was Jacqueline. He had to warn her. She had to escape. There was no need for them both to see their deaths.

Jonathan sent a signal. Jacqueline's ears went up like a radar. She could feel Jonathan running towards her. Something was wrong. She ran in his direction, "Jonathon!" she shouted! "What's wrong! What's happening!" She shouted as she turned the bend at the worst moment. She turned the bend just as the barn owl's claws landed on Jonathon. It grabbed him just at the back of his neck. Jonathon went limp. The barn owl flew away in a rage not even noticing that Jacqueline was there. "My Lord! My God! What has happened?" She thought. "Jonathan is gone!"

The Hard Move

Jacqueline's heart ached. She had never known such grief. She had to find a safe place, and it took all the strength she had to gather a few things and prepare to move. "My love has gone, and he didn't know we were having a little pup," She thought. Jacqueline spoke to the child she was carrying, "I'll find us a safe place." She remembered the manor she and Jonathon had passed by on their way to the barn. It was a few miles away. "There had to be plenty of food there," She thought. Off she went trekking through the snow and wind seeking shelter at Palouse Manor.

Jacqueline had been walking for what seemed like days when she came across Smidge eating nuts and corn. Smidge was a Mangalitsa (pronounced mahn-ga-leets-ah) pig. She was shipped to America from Hungary. Hungary is a land in central Europe. Mangalitsa pigs are quite different. They have lots of curly hair like sheep and live off the land eating grass, nuts, acorns, and such. Smidge hated the mud. She lived in a clover field all to herself. She was Olivia's favorite pet. Since it was winter, all the clover was gone. Olivia made sure Smidge had plenty of hay, a huge storage of nuts and fresh water every day.

"Who are you? and What are you doing in my clover field?" Smidge asked.

"There're no clovers here." Jacqueline smarted back. "It's winter."

"Well, In the spring there will be plenty of clover. Besides that, what are you doing out trekking in the snow? The winter moves have been over for months now. What are you doing? Why do you look so sad?"

Jacqueline sighs and tells in detail all the things that led up to her trekking in snow during the coldest part of the year and ending up in Smidges' now dead clover field. Smidge was smitten. She immediately had compassion, great care, for Jacqueline.

"You poor, poor dear. What a terrible thing to happen to you. Poor Jonathon, do you think there is any way he could have gotten away from the barn owl?" Smidge asked.

"I don't think so, Smidge. I don't think so at all." Jacqueline sighed.

"Come, come lay here underneath all of my fluffy hair." Smidge says. "It will keep you nice and warm. Tomorrow you'll meet Olivia. I'm sure she'll let you live in Palouse Manor. Once I tell her about the little pup, she'll be more than happy to let you stay."

"Tell her about my pup. What do you mean? You can't talk to a human." Jacqueline insists.

"You can talk to Olivia!" Smidge says with great excitement. "She has newair. Humans with newair can hear animal's thoughts as they travel on the wind."

"Wow, I've always heard of humans that can hear with newair. I've just never met one." Jacqueline says.

"Olivia loves animals, but sometimes she is so caught up in play she doesn't hear clearly. Sometimes it takes a lot of wind for her to hear. She always hears me though. I'm her favorite of all the animals on the farm."

"How is it that you're Olivia's favorite, Smidge?" Jacqueline asked.

"Well, Olivia wanted a pet. The farmers had already brought us Mangalitsa pigs over for food." Smidge explains.

"Oh my, Smidge, for food?" Jacqueline asked.

"Don't be sad Jacqueline. We understand our purpose." Smidge explains. "Anyway, Mangalitsa pigs are easy to farm. We search for our own food, and we eat nuts, leaves, and berries. The best thing is we don't have to live in muddy pigpens. I hate the mud. I'll never live in the mud! I prefer the clover." Smidge explains. "It nice and soft and smells so good in the spring.

When Olivia spotted me, it was love at first sight. I was soft gray with dark gray stripes. More than anything she loved my curly fluffy hair. Olivia comes by every day and brushes it. See how fluffy it is. That's how I like it best."

"I like you Smidge." Jacqueline declared. "It's nice and cozy underneath your belly too."

"I know. You just stay there and rest. Eat as many nuts as you want. I'll help you break the shells if you'd like. In the meanwhile, get your rest. In the morning we meet Olivia."

Olivia

The morning was bright and sunny. The sky was bright blue, and the wind was nice, steady, and crisp. It was exactly right for the animal's thoughts to travel on.

"Olivia, good morning!" exclaimed Smidge. "I have a pleasant surprise for you today…"

Before Smidge could finish her sentence, Olivia interrupts. She hears something. She could hear in a small faint whisper, "I hope she likes me. I hope she lets me stay in the manor."

"Who is that, Smidge? Who keeps saying I hope she likes me.?

Smidge nudges Jacqueline and tries to get her to stop thinking so loud. The wind was sharp and crisp today. Oliva could hear their thoughts easily.

"Don't tell her to be quiet, Smidge" Olivia says reaching her hand out for Jacqueline to crawl up on.

"Who are you little one?" she asks. "Why do you look so sad?"

Immediately Jacqueline's thoughts began to travel on the air to Olivia. It was as if the very air lifted Olivia and walked her through every terrible thing Jacqueline and poor Jonathon had suffered.

"Are you sure he didn't get away? Olivia asked. "You know barn owls don't usually fly away. As soon

as they catch you, they eat you."

"My goodness. I was in such a rush and feared so great for my life and my little pup that I ran. I ran as fast as I could." Jacqueline began to cry, "I... I never thought once to go back and look to see if Jonathon was safe. O my...what if he wasn't dead? What if he's alive? I am a horrible wife."

"There, there little one." Olivia says while softly rubbing Jacqueline's head and cheek. "You are no such thing. You are a great wife and will be a great mother. Jonathon would have wanted you to run away. He would definitely have wanted you to run away with his little pup."

Olivia loved Jacqueline. She placed her into her side pocket and carried her to class. "You'll be safe with me Jacqueline! Misty will never know you're here."

Meet the Smithsonians

When Olivia burst through the manor doors, we knew something was different, quite different. We Smithsonians' could tell a mouse was in the house.

"Smiths!" Olivia yelled. "Smiths come here! Kitties come quickly." She yelled quietly. We ran towards Olivia as she ran towards us.

Olivia paid close attention to Jacqueline who was hiding in her wide side pocket. Olivia held her softly as she ran. We almost ran into each other from the excitement.

"Olivia! What is all this noise?" Governess Misty cried out from the study which happened to be several rooms away. This was a good thing, because had she been around when Olivia so joyously pulled Jacqueline from her side pocket, she would have run in circles, grabbed a broom and fainted.

"This, my dear Smiths, is my new pet Jacqueline!"

"A mouse in the house!" We all yelled at once. Momma Smith was extremely nervous. "Mice bite up things. They eat and chew through everything," she thought, "How will we ever keep her a secret?"

"Smiths!" Olivia exclaimed. "Say hello! Stop being so rude to my friend."

"Hello Jacqueline," Momma Smith said in an

extremely nervous way. She tried to smile, but inside she was very worried.

"Hello Jacqueline," Poppa Smithsonians said as he comforted Momma.

I, baby Smith, was delighted. "Hi Jacqueline! Welcome to Palouse Manor. We're going to have lots of fun."

"Olivia," said Poppa Smith. "One of the conditions of our covenant is to keep the Manor free of mice. You're asking us to go against what we've been brought here to do."

"Don't be nervous Smith's," Olivia reassures, "I will keep Jacqueline a complete secret from Misty. I'll feed her and make sure she has a safe place to sleep and play. She's already met Smidge. Smidge can help me with her whenever I have to go into town with Misty to see dad. I would never ask you to break your promise to my dad to protect Palouse Manor, but Jacqueline is different. She is going to have a baby. She has lost her husband. We must keep her safe."

"Olivia!" Misty called. "Are you going to be late for my class today?"

"No way!" shouted Olivia, "I'm on my way now."

"Smith's," Olivia said under her breath, "We can do this. Jacqueline will be a perfect guest in our home. We must protect her. You'll never know that she's here!"

Class for Olivia went the same as it did so many times before. Misty drilled her on multiplication first thing in the morning.

"Five times one," Misty stated.

"Five," answered Olivia.

"Five times two."

"Ten!"

"Five times three."

"Fifteen!"

This went on all the way through the twelves. All the while little Jacqueline took in all the knowledge she could. She sat as quiet as only a mouse could be and recited her multiplication along with Olivia not fully understanding what it meant.

Olivia was always given a break in between lessons. "Okay Olivia," said Governess Misty, "You've done very well on your multiplication. You've been practicing. Take your break, and we'll go right into spelling after you come back."

"Whew," Olivia exhaled while looking at Jacqueline, "You'd think I wouldn't have to recite the entire multiplication table every day!"

"What is multiplication?" Jacqueline asked.

"Multiplication is a faster way to add numbers."

"What are numbers? What is adding?"

"My goodness Jacqueline, you are inquisitive. "Inquisitive, I-n-q-u-i-s-i-t-i-v-e, inquisitive, to ask many questions, to investigate. It's one of my new vocabulary words."

Olivia began to write the numbers one through ten on a sheet of paper. Jacqueline started to understand very quickly. In fact, she understood numbers and counting before Olivia's spelling lesson which began thirty minutes later.

Spelling became Jacqueline's most favorite subject. After her lessons Olivia spent the rest of the day teaching Jacqueline the alphabet.

Jacqueline spent hours scratching the alphabet into the walls. She even learned how to spell. It was her heart's desire to learn how to talk to all humans. It appeared that spelling and writing would be her way of doing so since most humans didn't have new air.

Jacqueline found a secret way into the walls of the manor. She spent hours scratching the alphabet into the walls. She was good at spelling. She once wrote an entire sentence on the wall. It was so small that to humans it looked like mouse scrapes. It wasn't. It was a complete sentence that said, "I am Jacqueline, and I am here.

Jacqueline lived in Palouse Manor for quite a while. She enjoyed music, learning, eating delicious food and running along the soft carpet. It was great for her. Poppa Smiths couldn't dare stop Jacqueline from learning. He would always say, "There must be a plan for her."

When the baby was born, we were all so excited. We didn't even realize he was here, until Olivia brought both Jacqueline and the baby in to see us. Tigger was so tiny. You could barely see his eyes. He yawned a lot. Like a little tiger. I immediately had a great idea. "Let's call him Tigger," I asked with great excitement.

"Tigger," said Jacqueline. "I like that. I like that a lot. Tigger the mouse."

"Hi little Tigger," Jacqueline said with great love, "Your daddy Jonathon would be very happy to see this day."

The Big Battle

It was Christmas Eve, and the weather was colder than ever. The snow was so high it had piled up to the porch. The wind howled like it was being whipped by God. It was warm inside though. Tigger and Jacqueline lay safely in the middle of the Smithsonians sleeping.

Later that night there was a loud commotion in the kitchen. Pots and pans rambled as feet ran quickly across the floor. Poppa Smith rushed to his feet to see what it was all about. Momma followed close behind, but I stayed with Jacqueline and Tigger.

It was bad. It was more than bad. Three roof rats had found their way into the manor. They were a bad bunch. The leader was a long lean fellow with gray and brown hair that was matted and shedding. His tail was twice as long as his body. Wrapped in his tail was a huge piece of bread he had clawed off the freshly baked loaf that sat on the counter.

The other two roof rats were round and pudgy with light brown hair. They sat there eating to their heart's content. They did not notice when Poppa Smith walked through the door.

Poppa Smith went into attack mode. Seeing roof rats in the manor caught him off guard. He never expected to find roof rats in his kitchen. Poppa growled and the roof rats immediately became afraid.

"No worries my friend," stated the leader of the pack, "we were just hungry." All the while he backed

away from Poppa towards the pet door the we use to get in and out of the manor.

"Please don't eat us," shouted the two round roof rats as they scurried out of the kitchen.

Momma Smith took off after them, leaving Poppa Smith to capture the leader. They were pudgy, but quick. They darted quickly into the living room. As fast as lightning they ran underneath the sofa, then underneath the coffee table. Momma Smith had to get a better look to see where the unwanted guests were headed. She leaped onto the living room chair, scattering the newspaper Misty had left earlier. It flew up into the air and landed all over the floor.

"There you are" she hissed. Momma Smith dashed into the hallway. It looked as if she was flying through the air. With one huge pounce she landed on the tip of the tail of one of the pudgy guests. "Meooowwww," Momma Smith yelped, "Now I've got you!"

The plump pudgy roof rat whimpered and hissed loudly. In fact, it was too loud. Misty came running from her bedroom into the hallway. Misty was the last person they wanted to know about the rats being in the house. She was so terribly afraid of them.

"Argggg!" yelled Misty, "What is that! Is that a rat? Is that a filthy fat roof rat?" She turned and ran down the hallway back into her room jumping into her bed with a single bound. She reached for her phone, but her hands were trembling, and she kept dropping it. "Rats! Filthy rat!" she kept repeating as she finally calmed her fingers to dial Olivia's dad. "Olivia, Olivia, I'm calling your dad right away. Our home has been taken over by rodents of the worst kind dear. Don't leave your room. It's awful out there!"

Olivia came running out of her room just in time to see the second pudgy roof rat make a dash for the bathroom.

"What in the world is going on out here?" Olivia's new air starts to pick up everything. All the animals are terrified. The Smiths were fighting, roof rats were afraid. "Oh my," she yells as she puts on her slippers. Just as she comes out of her room, she sees a round roof rat making a run for the bathroom. He runs so fast he hits the wall with a thud knocking himself unconscious.

"Now I've got you," she says as she traps him underneath the trash can. She immediately hurries back into the hallway where Momma Smith still had the first

pudgy roof rat in her mouth. He was terrified and crying big crocodile tears as Momma Smith carried him back into the kitchen. Olivia followed close behind her.

In the kitchen, Poppa Smith was fighting the fight for his life. The leader of the roof rats had managed to scratch him deeply above his right eye. The scratch caused Poppa Smith to have blurry vision. Despite it all Poppa Smith was not backing down. He had defended the manor too long to allow roof rats to take over.

There was hissing and yelping. Pots and pans dropped and were knocked around. There wasn't a place in the kitchen that had not gone untouched. The skinny roof rat dashed from one counter to the next, and Poppa Smith was right on his trail. There was a splash from a fork that the skinny roof rat knocked over into the dish water.

Poppa Smith came to a stop. He and the skinny roof rat stood face to face on the front edge of the kitchen sink. How they'd managed to end up there was beneath me. Momma Smiths' eyes widened with fear, but she did not let go of the first pudgy roof rat that was trapped in her mouth. Tigger and Jacqueline had woken, and they stood watching in fear. Everyone there knew Poppa Smith hated water, and the kitchen sink was full of it. Misty had left her dish water in the sink after cleaning up from dinner.

The skinny roof rat realized Poppa Smiths' fear and ran towards him. This startled Poppa Smith, and he lost his balance. His eyes were so blurry from his cut. He fell sideways and water splashed everywhere. Poppa Smith gasped. He knew it wasn't enough water to drown in, but it took his breath anyway. Tigger and Jacqueline scurried up to the countertop to help him.

The skinny leader roof rat turned his face towards Momma Smith. Momma Smith was not about to let

go of his friend. Her eyes widened as she thought about how if she dropped his friend, she would have to fight them both off. She had to protect the manor. The skinny leader roof rat came in for the fight. He was squeaking and clawing at Momma Smith, and she clawed back fiercely.

Momma Smith clawed at his head, and the skinny leader fell hard. Immediately, he jumped back up and ran towards Momma Smith again, but she was ready. The skinny roof rat ran hard and jumped into the air hoping to land on Momma Smiths head. He almost did, but Momma Smith struck him right in the belly. His arms flew into the air as he cartwheeled backwards smacking his head against the kitchen door.

Momma Smith ran towards him ready to attack again, but she was stopped in her tracks by the head of Smidge trying to get through the pet door flap. "Hey," yelled Smidge, "what in the world is going on in here?" All the fighting stopped. The Smithsonian's knew Smidge never left her clover field, and she was usually sleeping this time of night. The roof rats couldn't tell what Smidge was. They had never seen a curly haired pig. The roof rats were scared to death. They thought Smidge was an oversized cat!

Suddenly, the most amazing sight appeared as Smidge moved her fluffy head out of the way. There stood one worn and ragged mouse with a smile from ear to ear.

"Is Jacqueline here?" Jonathon asked as proper and humble as he could.

Momma Smith dropped the pudgy roof rat.

Jacqueline's heart started to beat twice as fast, as she rubbed her eyes in disbelief.

"Jonathon!" Jacqueline yelled as she ran towards him.

Jonathon stood there still very weak and tired from his trip. Somehow, he mustered up the strength to grab hold of his love Jacqueline.

"Jacqueline, I have searched for you so long my love." Jonathon whispered into her ear.

It was a happy reunion. Everyone sat in tears glaring at the two of them.

The roof rats saw a chance to escape. No one cared to stop them. Two loves had been united.

Suddenly Tigger snuggled in between his mom and dad. Jonathon almost fainted. "Is this my son?" he asked, knowing the answer all along.

"Yes, it is dear," she responded.

Tigger was so happy. He ran circles around his mom and dad dancing and singing. Everyone was so happy.

Suddenly, there was a loud yell followed by a loud thump. Olivia took off for the hallway bathroom. Everyone else walked carefully after her. Just as they entered the hallway, they saw Olivia coming out of the bathroom. She was carrying the trash can with the second pudgy roof rat inside. Misty had seen him and fainted on the bathroom floor.

Olivia opened the kitchen door to let the pudgy roof rat go to safety. The air was strong, and it blew inside allowing her to speak to the animals.

"I have to get you all to safety. It's not safe here. Misty called the exterminator. She also told my father to bring traps and poison to kill the rodents. It's just not safe for you to stay inside the manor any longer."

Jacqueline was heartbroken. She could not bear to take her son into the cruel world. Jonathan sighed heavily. He was still too weak to take care of his family.

"I have a solution!" shouted Poppa Smith, "We will keep Tigger here. We will take him everywhere he needs to go. We'll feed him our food only. He's a good child, and he will do as we tell him. We can keep him from harm. Do you trust us to do that Jacqueline, Jonathan?"

"Of course, we do Poppa Smith," said Jacqueline, "There is no one else I would trust more."

"Great, Jacqueline! That is wonderful!" said Poppa Smith.

"Jonathon, you and Jacqueline can stay with me," said Smidge. "I'll keep you nice and warm, and I have plenty of food."

"I will come visit you every day," said Poppa Smith, "I'll bring Tigger too."

"I will make sure this works, and we stay a happy family," said Olivia.

"That is a great idea," said Jonathon, "I think that will be absolutely perfect!"

The next day was Christmas, and everyone had already received the best gift ever. Jonathan was home with Jacqueline, and Tigger had his dad.

Nicole Mangum

Author – and CEO of Liberation's Publishing
www.liberationspublishing.com
nicole@liberationspublishing

Printed in the USA
CPSIA information can be obtained
at www.ICGtesting.com
LVHW092336141123
763949LV00001B/1